CHAPTER 2

Charlotte Herman

Illustrated by
Cat Bowman Smith

A Redfeather Book

Henry Holt and Company | New York

For Michael
who trusted me
with all his magic secrets

First edition
Published by Henry Holt and Company, Inc.,
115 West 18th Street, New York, New York 10011.
Published simultaneously in Canada by Fitzhenry & Whiteside Ltd.,
91 Granton Drive, Richmond Hill, Ontario L4B 2N5.

Library of Congress Cataloging-in-Publication Data
Herman, Charlotte.
Max Malone the Magnificent / Charlotte Herman;
illustrated by Cat Bowman Smith.
(A Redfeather book)
Summary: After seeing the Great Butoni perform at the local
public library, Max decides he wants to become a magician.
ISBN 0-8050-2282-1
[1. Magicians—Fiction.   2. Humorous stories.]   I. Smith, Cat
Bowman, ill.   II. Title.   III. Series: Redfeather books.
PZ7.H4313Mg   1993   [Fic]—dc20   92-14123

Printed in the United States of America on acid-free paper. ∞
1   2   3   4   5   6   7   8   9   10

Contents

Mystic Magic Set

"I am Max Malone the Magnificent," said Max Malone. "Watch closely as I place this red scarf inside my magic box, pass my magic wand over it, and presto change-o! The red scarf has become blue."

"Bravo! Bravo!" the audience shouted.

"That was wonderful," said Max's mother, applauding. Max took a bow.

"I'm pretty sure I know how you did that," said his sister, Rosalie. "But tell me anyway."

"A real magician never reveals his secrets," said Max. "And now for my next trick."

"Don't say *trick*," said Rosalie. "A real magician doesn't do tricks. He performs illusions."

"And now for my next illusion," Max continued, "I will make my sister disappear."

"Very funny," said Rosalie. "I'm just trying to help you succeed as a magician."

"You just succeeded in breaking the magic spell," said Max. He picked up all his tricks and packed them away in his Mystic Magic set. His mother had given it to him just a couple of days ago, but he already knew how to do most of the fifty tricks inside.

Among the tricks in the set were handcuffs to escape from, a color-changing rope, a vanishing coin, and tricks to defy gravity, like the incredible floating vase. There was a secret instruction book and a silver-speckled table where Max could set up his props.

"This is a great set," he told his mother. "Thanks for buying it for me. And it wasn't even my birthday."

"I knew you'd like it," said Mrs. Malone. "All you've talked about since your visit to the library is how you want to become a magician. I think this is a good way to start."

Last Saturday, Max and his best friend, Gordy, had gone to the public library to watch the Amazing Butoni perform his magic feats. Butoni, wearing a black tuxedo, produced bowls of fire and white doves from scarves. He even made a silver ball float mysteriously in the air.

For Max, the best part of the show was at the end. Butoni covered the dove cage with a large cloth, threw it into the air, and made the entire cage—doves and all—disappear.

The worst part of the show was Rosalie. She and a girlfriend turned up and sat behind them, trying to figure out how each trick was done. While everyone else sat mystified, saying "Ooh" and "Ahh," Rosalie kept saying "Simple. Easy. Nothing to it."

But what really bothered him was when Rosalie volunteered to be an assistant. She waved wildly to Max from the magician's platform. Max sank down in his chair and pretended he didn't know her.

But in spite of Rosalie, the show was fantastic. And right then and there, Max knew that he wanted to be a magician too. It might be a while before he could do the tricks—perform the illusions—that Butoni had done. But Max was a fast learner. It wouldn't take long. One day, with a little luck and a black tuxedo, he, Max Malone, would be known around the world as Max Malone the Magnificent. He'd be second only to the great Houdini.

Max Gets Hired

*H*arry Houdini didn't have Rosalie for a sister. If he had, he never would have become a great magician.

Rosalie was such a nag. Every time Max did a trick, Rosalie asked how it was done. Max always told her the same thing, "A real magician never reveals his secrets."

And Rosalie always answered, "He's permitted to reveal secrets to a family member."

So when Max made a tiny ball disappear from a tiny vase and Rosalie asked, "How did you do that, Max?" he gave her a different answer.

"You don't want to know."

"Yes, I do."

"It'll spoil the effect for you."

"No, it won't. I promise."

Finally Max gave in. He showed her the secret compartment where the ball was hidden.

"Oh, is that all there is to it?" she asked. "Big deal."

But Gordy never asked Max to reveal his secrets. Neither did Austin Healy. Austin Healy was Max's neighbor from across the street. He was just six years old, but Max liked him anyway. He was the only kid Max knew who was named after a car.

Gordy and Austin were a good audience to perform for. They laughed and applauded for Max every time he did one of his tricks from his Mystic Magic set. And they never wanted to know how the tricks were done.

"Don't tell me how anything's done," said Austin. "It'll spoil the illusion. I like to believe in magic."

"Me too," said Gordy. "It was bad enough finding out there's no such thing as Santa Claus. Or the tooth fairy. There's got to be some magic left in the world."

"No tooth fairy?" asked Austin, looking glum.

"Well," said Gordy, "there might be a tooth fairy. I'm not sure about that one."

"I think the tooth fairy is still around," said Max. And he hurried to do another trick so he could get Austin's mind on something else.

"You're really good at this," said Austin when Max changed a plain piece of paper into a dollar bill. "You could perform at birthday parties and charge money. You've even got a magic table. It makes you look like a real magician."

"That's a great idea," said Max.

"You could make a lot of money," said Gordy. "I bet you could charge five dollars a show."

"Easy," said Austin. "My mother pays more than that for a clown. Every year I have a clown for my birthday party. But I'm sick of clowns. I'm too old for them. I'd rather have a magician at my next party. I'd rather have you, Max. I was going to invite you guys anyway."

Austin was going to invite them? To a party for six- and seven-year-olds? Max didn't know how he felt about being at a party with a lot of little kids. But as long as he would be there as a magician, it didn't matter.

"When's your party?" Max asked.

"In about three weeks. Will you do it, Max? Will you do magic for my party?"

"Sure. If it's okay with your mother."

"When I tell her you're charging five dollars, I know it'll be okay."

"In a few months you can entertain at my party too," said Gordy. "My mother will say yes for sure. She goes nuts at my parties. She says there's nothing harder than trying to keep a bunch of boys entertained. My father will say yes too. He likes quality entertainment. And magic is quality."

Max couldn't believe what was happening. He had hardly begun to do magic, and he already had two shows lined up. He was becoming a professional magician sooner than he had expected.

To do something fun. Something that you love doing. And to get paid for it. What could be better than that?

"Double-check with your mother," Max told Austin. "And then three weeks from now, I'll be ready."

3

The Magic Factory

"**W**hat do you mean, you've outgrown your magic set?" Mrs. Malone asked Max. "You've had it for just a week. There are fifty tricks in that set. Plus a magic table. How could you outgrow it so fast?"

Max's mother, who sold personalized memo pads and address labels through the mail, had just completed a fairly large order. Max thought this would be a good time to approach her with his request.

"Well, I didn't outgrow it, exactly," said Max. "I've just sort of moved on. If I'm going to do Austin's party, I'll need some bigger illusions."

Mrs. Healy had agreed to have Max perform at Austin's party. She said the price was right.

"I'll be performing in front of a large audience,"

Max went on. "Not only little kids, but parents, too. I can't just work out of my magic set. I need a few bigger illusions to round out my routine."

"You have a routine?" asked Mrs. Malone.

"Well, not yet. But I'm going to plan one. I thought I'd go to the magic store first and see what they have."

"How much will your new routine cost me?" Mrs. Malone asked.

"Not a penny," said Max. "I still have all that birthday money you almost never let me use."

"I keep telling you, Max. I'm saving it for college."

"But if you let me have it now, you can think of it as an investment."

"An investment?"

"An investment in my future as a magician. Or a loan. I'll make up the money in no time by doing birthday parties. I've already got ten dollars coming to me."

Max's mother looked off into space. She seemed to be staring at the seams in the wallpaper.

"I'll tell you what," she said. "If you buy just one trick at a time, and learn to do it before you buy another, I'll let you use some of your money. But I want you to choose your tricks wisely."

. . .

"I have to choose my tricks wisely," Max told Gordy on the way to the magic store. "I have a limited amount of money to spend."

"You have to look for quality magic at a good price," Gordy said.

After a long walk they finally reached the Magic Factory. WE SUPPLY AMERICA'S MAGIC was written across the window. Max had been there before to buy gag items—a squirting flower, a fake hand, and some other great stuff that he used to frighten or annoy Rosalie. But this was the first time he had entered the store as a magician.

It was a small store. Shelves of magic equipment and books lined most of the walls from floor to ceiling. Glass cases held gold and silver tubes and canisters. There were red boxes and black boxes, cups and balls, and scarves of all colors.

On another wall were magic posters showing some of the great magicians. There were magicians of the past—Harry Houdini, Adelaide Herrmann, Howard Thurston, and Harry Blackstone. And there were some of the great magicians of today—Doug Henning, David Copperfield, and Siegfried and Roy.

Max could just imagine a poster of himself as Max Malone the Magnificent. He'd be wearing a black tuxedo while floating a silver ball in the air. Or producing white doves from colored scarves.

"Look," said Gordy, pointing to a shelf. "Isn't that the set you have?"

"Yeah, the good old Mystic Magic set. This is where my mother bought it."

"You've outgrown your magic set and now you're ready for something greater," came a voice.

Max looked up to see an old lady walk out from the back room. He remembered her as the same one who had sold him the gag items some time ago.

"You want a bigger trick," she went on. "Something you can do in front of a large audience."

"Yeah," said Max. Was this lady some kind of mind reader? he wondered. "I'm doing a birthday party soon. I need a good trick."

"A quality trick at a good price," Gordy offered.

"Maybe I can help you," said the lady. "But could you wait for just a minute? I've suddenly become very thirsty." She turned and went back into the other room. Soon she was out again carrying a pitcher of milk.

"A whole pitcher?" Max whispered to Gordy. "Gee, she must really be thirsty."

"I'll be with you boys in a moment," she said.

Max watched as she poured some milk into a red plastic cup and set the pitcher on a table. Holding her cup of milk, she walked toward Max and Gordy. "Now let's see how I can help you. Ooh . . . ooh!" She tripped, lost her balance, and lunged toward them, the cup tipping over in her hand. "Watch out!"

Max and Gordy ducked. But the milk had changed into confetti. And it was confetti that was raining down on them.

"Pretty good, huh?" said the lady, laughing.

"Wow! That was great," Max said, straightening up. "I've got to have that. That's the trick I want."

"It's a quality trick," said Gordy.

"I knew you'd like it," she said. "It's not too expensive and it's easy to learn. I recommend this trick to all my budding young magicians."

Max puffed out his chest. He liked to think of himself as a budding young magician. "I'll do it at Austin's party," he told Gordy.

"You can use a hat instead of a cup," the lady said.

"Or a newspaper. That's especially good in front of a large audience." She took a newspaper and showed Max how to roll it up in the shape of a cone. "The audience sees you pour milk into the cone. Then when you open the newspaper over their heads, they'll become hysterical."

"I'd like my audience to become hysterical," said Max.

"I also suggest that you buy some Moo."

"Moo?" Max asked.

"It's a powder that you mix with water. It looks just like milk. Of course it isn't. And you have to make sure no one drinks it. But it lasts a long time. And by using it you won't have to waste any real milk."

After Max paid for the disappearing-milk trick and the Moo, the lady gave him a catalog from the Magic Factory so he could study the kinds of tricks that were available.

"I'll help you pick out another trick," said Gordy on the way home.

"Thanks," said Max. "But first I have to learn the milk trick. I'll practice it on my practice audience. I can't wait to make everyone hysterical."

Practice Audience

*T*he audience held its breath as Max Malone the Magnificent walked toward it with a newspaper cone filled with milk. Max held the cone directly over Rosalie's head. She became hysterical.

"Don't you dare, Max! No, Max, don't!" she screamed.

Everyone shrieked and ducked as Max opened the newspaper and let confetti pour over them. They all breathed a sigh of relief. Especially Rosalie.

"That was wonderful," said Mrs. Malone. "I thought for sure I was going to get splattered with milk."

"That was the greatest," said Austin Healy. "You've got to do that one at my party."

"How did you do it?" asked Rosalie.

"Forget it," Max answered.

"You sure learned that trick fast," said Gordy when he and Max were alone and ready to look through the catalog.

"It was easy," said Max.

"In no time you'll be as good as the Amazing Butoni. You'll be able to perform at the library."

"You can be my assistant," said Max. He turned to page one of the catalog.

Welcome to the Wonderful World of Magic

You are now the lucky owner of magic's greatest and most complete catalog. As in the past, we will offer you the finest in magical illusions and apparatus.

Remember—a valuable part of every magic effect is its secret. So choose with care. Once you have learned the secret, books and tricks cannot be returned.

Prices are subject to change without notice.

"I'd better choose with care," said Max. "I've got to give this lots of thought."

It was hard for Max to concentrate with Rosalie in the next room. She was singing "The hills are alive with the sound of music" into her tape recorder. The song was from an old movie—*The Sound of Music*— that she had seen on TV the other night. Rosalie loved old movies. The older the better.

"She thinks she's Julie Andrews," Max told Gordy. "Ever since she sang at Austin's carnival, she thinks she's a professional. She wants to try out for 'Star Search.'"

"I remember," said Gordy. "She sang the whole score of *South Pacific*."

"She sounds better outside," Max said, closing the door to his room. "Okay, now, let's see what new magic I should buy."

The catalog was filled with the most wonderful tricks—card tricks, rope tricks, and coin tricks. There was a cane that could change into a scarf. A needle that could pierce a balloon without breaking it. And a vanishing bowl of water.

"There's so much to choose from," said Max. "How is anyone supposed to know what to buy? And some of the stuff is really expensive."

"How about this newspaper trick?" Gordy suggested. "You rip up a page from a newspaper into a bunch of little pieces and put it back together again. And it doesn't cost a lot because you just buy the instructions."

Max thought about the newspaper trick all the way to the Magic Factory.

"The newspaper trick is a good choice," he said to Gordy as they entered the shop. "I saw it done on TV once."

Today there were two people in the shop: the old lady behind the counter, and an old man in front of it. The man was wearing plaid pants and a striped shirt.

"Well, hello again," said the lady. "How did that last trick work out?"

"I made my sister hysterical," said Max.

The man was fiddling with a coin and made it disappear. He pulled another coin out of the air and made that disappear too.

"How can I help you today?" the lady asked Max.

"I want to buy instructions for the newspaper trick."

"The torn and restored newspaper," Gordy explained.

"I wouldn't buy that if I were you," said the man, removing a coin from Max's ear.

"Why not?" asked Max.

"Walter, you're doing it again," said the lady.

"Doing what again?" asked Walter.

"Talking a customer out of buying something."

"Now, Fran, you know that trick isn't as easy as it looks. It takes an awful lot of practice. He needs lots of experience."

"Even so, it's not your place to discourage business."

"Come on, Fran, I was only trying to—"

"I don't care what you were trying to do. Just don't do it anymore. Do you hear me?" Her voice grew louder. "I'm sick of having you hanging around here ruining my business. Sick, sick, sick!"

Max and Gordy exchanged worried glances.

What was going on? Max heard adults yell at kids all the time. Especially a couple of teachers he could think of. But he had never heard one adult yelling at another like that.

"Chill out, Fran," said Walter.

"Don't tell me to chill out, you . . . you . . ." She

cracked an egg into a blue plastic glass, walked over to Walter, and turned it over on his head.

Max and Gordy cringed. Max could barely make himself look at Walter when Fran removed the glass. He didn't want to see gooey, slimy—flowers! A whole bouquet of flowers appeared on top of Walter's head.

Walter and Fran burst out laughing.

After breathing sighs of relief Max and Gordy laughed along with them.

"Great," said Max. "That was great. Do you think I could do that one?"

"Sure," said Walter. "As the instructions say, there's no skill required. But like all magic, it does take some practice."

"And the price is reasonable," Fran added.

"I want the newspaper trick too," said Max.

"Walter is right about that one," said Fran. "It's hard to learn. I'd advise you to wait awhile before you buy it."

Max really wanted that trick. He had his heart set on it. "I think I'll give it a try anyway," he said. Then over his shoulder he whispered to Gordy, "I still have two whole weeks to learn it."

Max paid for his magic. And while Fran put everything in a bag, Walter pulled coins out from behind Max's and Gordy's ears. Max knew that one day he would learn how to do that too.

"I thought you were supposed to buy just one trick at a time," said Gordy on the way home.

"The newspaper trick isn't really a trick. I just bought the instructions. And you heard what Walter said. The egg-to-flowers trick requires no skill. It won't take long to learn." Max quickened his pace. "Let's hurry, Gordy. I can't wait to present Rosalie with a bouquet of flowers."

Baby

"I'm sorry, I'm sorry," said Max. "I didn't mean to get egg all over your face."

"You rotten little monster, you!" screamed Rosalie, grabbing a towel.

"It was an accident," said Max. "Something went wrong."

Austin Healy and Gordy were rolling on the floor, laughing.

"Hey, you missed a spot," Max told Rosalie while she was wiping her face with the towel. And now he was laughing too.

"Sometimes tricks work better when they don't work," said Austin, clutching his stomach.

"I guess I need some practice," said Max.

Max also had to practice his newspaper trick. Every day he practiced tearing and folding, trying to understand the directions. They were hard to follow.

Directions are always hard to follow, Max thought. Once when he ordered Muscle Man from a cereal company, he couldn't put it together. It came in a lot of little pieces and easy-to-follow directions that weren't easy to follow.

When I grow up, he thought, I'll start a company that rewrites instructions so people can understand them.

■   ■   ■

One day after he had practiced his newspaper trick, Max decided to begin planning his routine for Austin's party. He would start with the disappearing-milk trick, do some smaller tricks from his Mystic Magic set, and then go on to the newspaper trick and egg to flowers.

He took a pencil and a sheet from his notepad that said *From the Desk of Max Malone* and wrote:

Routine for Austin's Party

Disappearing-milk trick
Paper to dollar bill
Color-changing scarf
Torn and restored newspaper
Egg to flowers

It looked like a good routine. Except that he knew it wouldn't take up a whole half hour. And that's how long Austin's mother wanted Max to perform. He needed to do something else. And it had to be something professional. Not another small trick from his magic set. He would have to go back to the Magic Factory. Maybe Fran or Walter—if he was there— would have a suggestion.

Fran and Walter were both in the shop when Max walked in a short while later. This time Walter was behind the counter wearing striped pants and a plaid shirt. He was flipping a card between his fingers and made it disappear. Max hoped that Walter would teach him how to do that one day.

Fran was dusting the shelves with a feather duster. "How's our young magician coming along?" she asked Max.

"Pretty good," said Max. "I made my sister hysterical again."

"I was hoping you'd come by. I have a really good trick to show you."

Fran held up a square box and looked through it. Max could see her face on the other side.

"Good grief," she said. "There's no bottom to this box. Our builder forgot to put one on." She picked up another box. A smaller one. She looked through that one too. "No bottom on this one either. I can't believe it."

Walter shook his head. "They don't make 'em like they used to."

Fran placed the smaller box inside the larger one. "I guess I'll have to show you the trick another day. I'll get my builder to . . . wait a minute. What's this?"

She put her hand inside the box and pulled out a red scarf that was tied to a yellow one that was tied to a blue one. The blue one was tied to a green one that was tied to a white one and a purple one and a pink one. She pulled out scarf after scarf, until she had a whole pile of them on the counter. She put her hand back inside and pulled out yards and yards of ribbon and paper chains and round metal rings that were linked together. And last of all, a large rubber chicken.

Max stood there with his mouth open. He was speechless. Finally he found his voice. "Where did all that stuff come from? Both of the boxes were empty. I saw them."

"This is our number-one production illusion," said Fran. "You can produce a huge amount of fun stuff from it. And there's no skill required."

"I've got to have it," said Max. But when she told him the price, he knew he couldn't buy it.

"It's too expensive," he said. "I don't have that much money."

"You don't have to buy it," said Fran. "For one dollar we can sell you the construction plans. It's not that hard to build. In fact, you can make lots of your own magic illusions."

"Or you can do magic with cards and coins," said Walter, pulling a card out of the air. "We've got all kinds of books that will teach you how. Or you can get them at the library and it won't cost you a cent. Why, some very great magicians have done only card and coin magic."

"I can learn about cards and coins after Austin's party," said Max. "Right now I have to do tricks with no skill required."

Max paid for his instructions and turned to leave. That's when he saw it. On a table in a corner of the store sat the cutest, smallest white rabbit he had ever seen. It was sitting in a cage, washing its face with its paws—just like a kitten.

Max smiled when the rabbit did that.

"Her name is Baby," said Walter. "She looks like a baby rabbit, but she's full grown. That's because she's a dwarf rabbit. She'll never get any bigger."

He took Baby out of her cage and held her against his chest. He stroked her head. "We've been doing magic together for two years. Haven't we, Baby? But I'm retired now—and thinking about giving her to a deserving young magician."

I'm a deserving young magician, thought Max. He'd love to have a rabbit like that.

"Someone who's kind to animals and will take good care of her."

I'm kind to animals, thought Max. And he was. He never threw rocks at squirrels. Or purposely stepped on anthills. And in the winter when snow covered the ground, he put out breadcrumbs for the birds.

"I'd take good care of her," said Max.

"Would you be able to keep her?" asked Walter. "Maybe you should check at home first."

"I'm pretty sure," said Max. "My mother is investing in my future as a magician."

Max wasn't sure at all. He remembered something about his mother being allergic to cats and dogs. But she had never said anything about being allergic to rabbits.

"Tell you what," said Walter. "If you promise to take real good care of her, I'll let you have her. Cage and all."

"I promise," said Max.

"But remember—if you can't keep her, or find a good home for her, you have to bring her back."

Walter gave Max lots of instructions in the care and feeding of Baby.

"Plenty of cuddling and plenty of exercise. Keep her water bottle filled. And feed her twice a day. Rabbit pellets and carrots. No lettuce."

"No lettuce?" Max asked.

"Lettuce can make a rabbit sick."

"No lettuce," said Max.

"She's even litter-box trained," said Walter.

"Really?" Max asked. "I didn't know you could train a rabbit for that."

Max held Baby in his arms and petted her. She was soft and warm. She felt like a small furry pillow. He loved the way she wiggled her nose when she looked at him.

Now, with a rabbit of his own, Max felt even more like a real magician. His mother had to let him keep Baby. She just had to.

Allergic

"A rabbit?" Mrs. Malone cried. "Max, this time you've gone too far. I was willing to go along with a few new tricks. But a rabbit?"

"Don't you know?" Rosalie asked him. "Mom's allergic."

"She's allergic to cats and dogs," Max corrected. "This is a rabbit."

"I'm allergic to any four-legged creature with hair," said Mrs. Malone. "I've already let you keep your cat. But two furry animals are too much. And that's beside the point. You have to ask me before you bring an animal into the house."

"But this isn't just any animal," Max argued. "It's

an experienced magic rabbit. And it's litter-box trained."

Max took Baby out of the cage and held her. "Her name is Baby. Isn't she cute?" Max held her so his mother could see the rabbit's nose wiggle.

"Oh, she really is adorable," said Mrs. Malone, petting the top of Baby's head. "But that's beside the point too," she added quickly. "With an animal comes responsibility. There's . . . *ah ah ah-choo*—the feeding. And the . . . *ah ah ah-choo*—the cleaning." She took a tissue and blew her nose. "I'm afraid you'll have to take her . . . *ah ah ah-choo*—back." She blew her nose again.

"But I have to have a rabbit," pleaded Max. "I'm a magician."

"You don't need a rabbit to be a magician," said Rosalie. "You can do card and coin magic."

"It isn't fair," said Max. He loved the little rabbit. He didn't want to give her back to Walter.

Suddenly Max had an idea. Even if he couldn't keep Baby, he didn't have to give her to Walter. He could give her to Gordy. Gordy was kind to animals. He would take good care of her. That's what mattered. And Max could play with her whenever he wanted to.

He put the rabbit back into her cage and ran to the phone. He punched in Gordy's number. He told him about Baby. "Can you keep her?" he asked.

"My father's allergic to animals," said Gordy.

Max punched in Austin's number. Austin was kind to animals too. He was kind to Newton, his red-spotted newt.

He told Austin about Baby. "Can you keep her?" he asked.

"I'll be right over," said Austin.

■ ■ ■

"You can play with her whenever you want to," Austin told Max. He was holding Baby and scratching the rabbit behind her ears. "And you can use her in your magic shows. Is she litter-box trained?"

"How did you know about litter-box training a rabbit?" Max asked. He showed Austin the small litter box inside the cage.

"I like animals," said Austin. "I read about them all the time."

"Are you sure you can keep her?" asked Max. "Is anyone in your family allergic?"

"My mother is allergic to cactus plants," said Austin. "They make her skin break out. But she's not allergic to animals. Neither is my father. They said I can keep her. She can live downstairs in our rec room. She'll have plenty of room to run around. And I'll give her lots of chew sticks so she won't chew on the furniture. But I won't give her any lettuce."

Austin really did know a lot about rabbits, Max thought.

After Austin left with Baby, Max started to work on his production illusion. He bought wood cut to size at the lumberyard. He spent the next few days hammering pieces together to form the right kinds of boxes with a secret compartment. He painted the boxes red and gold.

Finally it was finished. His production illusion was beautiful. Max thought it looked very professional. But would it work right?

He practiced loading the secret compartment with paper chains, his mother's scarves tied together, and

Rosalie's rubber ducky. The trick was pretty easy to do. And the effect was amazing.

Next Max practiced the newspaper trick. That was not so easy. For days he tore and folded pages of a newspaper. He couldn't get the trick to work. The torn pieces of paper always fell to the floor. He thought about asking Fran and Walter for help, but he didn't want them to say "We told you so." Maybe they were right. Maybe Max needed more experience.

Then one day, to Max's surprise, the trick worked. He tore a page from a newspaper into lots of small pieces. Then, using the secret method that he had learned, he restored it. The page was back the way it had been in the beginning. In perfect shape. All his practice had paid off.

It was another amazing illusion. And Max was thrilled. Fran and Walter would be surprised to hear that Max had been able to figure out how to do it.

With Austin's party less than a week away, it was time for Max to plan his revised routine. On a fresh sheet of paper from his notepad he wrote:

Routine for Austin's Party (Revised)

Disappearing-milk trick
Paper to dollar bill
Color-changing scarf
Torn and restored newspaper
Egg to flowers
Production illusion

Max glanced over the sheet one more time. He wanted to make sure he hadn't left anything out. But there they were. Six wonderful tricks.

"Looking good," said Max.

Patter

"There's something wrong with your act," said Rosalie. She was in the living room, watching Max practice his routine.

"What's wrong with it?" asked Max. He couldn't see anything wrong. All the tricks were working perfectly.

"It's your presentation," said Rosalie. "Something's missing."

"What do you mean?" asked Max.

"For one thing, you could use some good patter."

"I'm running out of money," said Max.

"Patter isn't something you buy," Rosalie explained. "It's the language you use when you're performing. It's part of your routine. For instance—

when you change the red scarf to blue, you don't have to say, 'I'm changing the red scarf to blue.' Your audience can see that. You have to say something clever. Like

> I can't let my mother do my laundry anymore. Everything she washes changes color. When she washes something red, it comes out . . . blue! Ta-da!

"See what I mean?"

"That's clever?" asked Max.

"It's a start," said Rosalie. "And you could use some music, too. And an assistant. I'd be happy to assist you. I even have my tutu left over from when I took ballet."

"Forget it," said Max. "This is supposed to be a magic show. Not a horror show. Anyway, I have enough to do without worrying about music and patter and tutus. I have to concentrate hard just to make the tricks come out right."

But Max couldn't concentrate with Rosalie around. She kept making up patter for him. When he changed the plain white paper to a dollar bill, she made up:

I never worry about money. Whenever I need
some, I put a blank piece of paper into my magic
money machine and out comes . . . a dollar bill!
Ta-da!

Rosalie also played song after song from her *Oldies
but Goodies* tape in order to pick out music for the
show.

Max had to get away from her. First he went to visit
Austin so he could check on the rabbit.

"Maxine Baby is a real magic rabbit," Austin told
him.

"Maxine Baby?"

"I wanted to name her after you, Max. But I didn't
want to take away her real name. She'd get confused.
So I call her Maxine Baby. Anyway, she's a real magician. She escapes from her cage. She knows how to
lift up the latch. She runs around the rec room and
comes back when she's hungry. Or thirsty. Or has to
use the litter box. Now we just leave her cage door
open, and she comes and goes."

"Where is she now?" Max asked. Maxine Baby
wasn't in her cage.

"Probably hiding in a small, dark place somewhere," said Austin. "She likes to do that."

After Max left Austin, he made another visit to the Magic Factory. He hoped to find one final trick to further round out his routine. What he found was a shiny silver floating ball. It was part of a collection of used magic that Fran had just bought. So it didn't cost much. It looked like the same kind of ball that Butoni had floated at the library.

Max bought a used snake can too. The outside of the can said *Peanut Brittle*. But when you took the top off, two spring "snakes" leaped out.

A surprise purchase was a tuxedo shirt-front that Walter let him have for half-price. It was white and had a black bow tie. Walter showed him how to wear it over his regular shirt by tying the elastic bands around his neck and waist.

"When you wear this under your suit jacket it looks like a real tux," he said.

Walter also gave Max some free advice. He was happy to give it after Max assured him that Baby was in good hands.

"Remember," said Walter. "It's not enough just to do the tricks. It's the way you do them. It's better to do one trick perfectly than to do ten of them sloppily. Your goal as a magician is to entertain your audience. The right music and patter can make the difference."

When Max got back home, Rosalie was still choosing music. He couldn't figure out how she knew so much about performing magic. But Rosalie always seemed to know everything. It bothered him that she knew about patter. And he didn't.

"Want some peanut brittle?" he asked her. He knew she would never say no to candy. Or anything sweet. She could eat sugared cereal by the box and never get sick of it.

"Oh, I love peanut brittle," she said.

Max aimed the top of the can in Rosalie's direction. He unscrewed the cover. The "snakes" leaped out, and Rosalie screamed.

"That's not funny! Pick out your own music!" She turned off her tape recorder and left the room in a huff.

"I was just using patter," Max called after her.

With Rosalie out of the way Max was able to concentrate on his show. He practiced the floating ball. Then he wrote out his new revised routine.

Routine for Austin's Party (New and Revised)

Disappearing-milk trick
Paper to dollar bill
Color-changing scarf
Snake can
Floating ball
Torn and restored newspaper
Egg to flowers
Production illusion

He looked over his list of tricks. He thought of the milk pitcher. And his audience becoming hysterical. He thought of the egg to flowers and everyone laughing beyond control. He thought of their amazement at the newspaper trick. And the production illusion. And the floating ball.

They were wonderful tricks. He had chosen wisely. And now, with his tuxedo shirt-front, Max Malone the Magnificent was ready!

The Magic Show

*I*t was the day of Austin's party. Gordy came over to help Max carry his magic equipment across the street to Austin's house. It took two trips to get everything there. Not only did Max have all those magic tricks to bring, he also had his magic table. And Rosalie's tape recorder. Max had recorded the theme song of "Bonanza" from the TV. He had had to watch a few days of old reruns to get enough music for his routine.

Then there was Austin's present. Max and Gordy had chipped in to buy him a new album for his baseball cards. Austin enjoyed collecting cards. He had so many of them that he was always running out of places to store them.

Mrs. Malone wished Max good luck. She gave him a brand-new memo pad. It said *Max Malone the Magnificent.* "It's to write down the names of all the new clients you're sure to get."

The show was planned for two o'clock, but Max and Gordy got to Austin's house early to set up.

"Happy birthday, Austin," said Max and Gordy. They handed Austin his gift.

"Wow, thanks," said Austin as he helped carry Max's magic down to the rec room. "We're having the magic show first. Then we'll have the cake and ice cream. And then the presents."

Max looked around at all the balloons and streamers decorating the room. A long table was covered with a Mickey Mouse tablecloth and matching paper plates and cups. There were Mickey Mouse party favors too. This was going to be a real party. A real magic show. And Max was going to be the star attraction. He gulped.

"Where's Maxine Baby?" Max asked, looking at the open cage. He wanted to hold the little rabbit. Pet her. Maybe he would feel less nervous.

"Probably in one of her favorite hiding places," said

Austin. "She'll come out sooner or later."

Austin showed Max where to set up. Max put most of the large magic tricks on a card table that Mrs. Healy had waiting for him. He placed the tricks from his Mystic Magic set on his small magic table. Everything else went on the floor.

The doorbell rang to announce the arrival of the first guest. Max's hands began to sweat. One by one, Austin's friends came down to the rec room. Each one handed Austin a present, then ran around the room. Some of the kids tried to peek at Max's tricks. But Gordy chased them away.

"Are you the magician?" one of them asked Max.

"Yes," said Max. He tried to sound professional. Sure of himself. But he wasn't sure at all.

After everyone had arrived, Mr. Healy called out, "Okay, everyone be seated. Our magic show is about to begin."

Max's heart thumped. He adjusted his bow tie.

All the kids scrambled for the best places on the floor. Right at Max's feet. Mr. Healy had to move them back. "Give the magician room to work," he told them.

Max looked out at the crowd. This was a real live audience. Not just a practice audience. It was one thing to perform in front of his mother and Rosalie. Or even Gordy and Austin. But it was something else to perform in front of so many strangers.

There were about fifteen kids sitting Indian style on the floor. Most were about Austin's age. But right in the middle there were two kids around four years old. Max wished they were all four years old. Then if he messed up, they wouldn't know the difference.

Austin's mother and father and a few other parents sat in chairs behind the kids. Max wished they'd go upstairs to have some coffee.

After the kids had quieted down, Austin got up from the floor.

"Welcome to my party, everyone. I want to present . . . for the very first time . . . Max Malone the Magnificent!"

The audience cheered and applauded. Some of the kids even knew how to whistle. Max froze. His mind went blank. He forgot what he was supposed to do. He couldn't remember his routine. He couldn't remember his patter.

He spotted Gordy across the room. Gordy made pouring motions. Good old Gordy. Max sprang into action.

He held up his milk pitcher filled with Moo. He remembered his patter.

"How many of you have had your milk today?" he asked. Most of the kids raised their hands. "Good," said Max, rolling a sheet of newspaper into a cone. "But for those of you who haven't, I have some for you." He poured the Moo into the cone and walked toward the audience.

He held the cone high up in the air and waved it over their heads. Kids shrieked and ducked and became hysterical as Max opened the paper and shook out the confetti.

The audience went wild. They clapped and cheered and whistled again. Max took a slight bow. Maybe he had nothing to worry about after all.

Next he did the paper-to-dollar-bill trick. He used the patter that Rosalie had given him. And when he changed the red scarf to blue, he used her patter too. After each trick the audience applauded. And Max bowed. Things were going well.

Then came the snake can. He had made up his own patter for this trick.

"One thing about doing magic, it really gets me hungry. Would anyone like some peanut brittle?"

All the kids waved their hands. Max turned the top of the can toward them. He unscrewed the cover and out leaped the "snakes."

Everyone screamed with delight. Everyone except the two four-year-olds. They just screamed. And cried. Two mothers came over and tried to get them to stop. But the kids only cried harder. Max was stunned. This wasn't supposed to happen. This was terrible.

He had to act quickly. He turned on the tape recorder. The "Bonanza" music would come on. He would do his floating ball trick. Then the kids would stop crying.

Max lifted up a large cloth. The silver ball peeked out from behind. Then the tape began to play "The hills are alive with the sound of music." Max was in shock. What was that? What happened to "Bonanza?" How did Rosalie get in there?

The kids started laughing. Max's hand shook. The

floating ball fell to the floor. When Max bent down to pick it up, the elastic band around his neck snapped. The top of his tuxedo shirt flipped forward. The kids roared.

Stop laughing! Max wanted to shout. This isn't funny.

Quickly Max reached for his next trick. The newspaper. He held the sheet in front of him.

"Watch closely as I tear up this paper into a million pieces," he said as he began tearing. "And now I will magically restore it. Ta-da!"

All the pieces of newspaper fell to the floor. Everyone was hysterical. Max wished he had never come here. The show was a total disaster.

Max Malone
the Magnificent

Max wished he were a real magician. Then he could make himself disappear. A puff of smoke, and he'd be gone. But he was still at Austin's party. And the audience was still laughing at him.

"You're great, Max!" Austin called out. "You're the funniest. You're the best comedian ever."

Funny? Comedian? What was Austin talking about? Max looked at the crowd. He saw all the laughing faces. They were having a good time.

Max brightened. "Austin," he called. "Go get me an egg."

By the time Austin came back with the egg, Max was ready with his blue plastic glass. He was ready with his patter too.

"Austin," Max began, "I want you to stand right here. Since we're celebrating your birthday today, I want to give you a special present."

He whispered something in Austin's ear. Austin smiled.

Max turned to the audience. "Heh, heh," he said, sneering his most evil sneer. He cracked the egg into the glass. Austin closed his eyes. The audience giggled.

Max walked right up to Austin, sneered at the audience again, and turned the glass over on Austin's head.

"Oh, gross!" the kids yelled. The four-year-olds sat wide-eyed, their mouths open.

"Abracadabra," said Max. "The egg has changed into flowers. Ta-da!" Max removed the glass. Egg poured down Austin's face.

The audience burst out laughing. Austin seemed to be laughing the hardest. Kids were rolling on the floor. Mrs. Healy, who was all smiles, brought Austin a towel to wipe his face.

Satisfied with his performance, Max went on to his last trick.

"And now for my last trick," Max announced. He lifted up his production illusion from the floor and set it on the table. To Rosalie's singing of "Climb Every Mountain," Max picked up the large box. He stuck his hand through it to show that it was empty. He did the same thing with the small one.

As Max placed the smaller box inside the larger one, a terrible thought came to him. He had forgotten to load the secret compartment. He had left the scarves, paper chains, and Rosalie's rubber ducky at home. He had nothing to produce. He couldn't even think of anything funny to do. How could he end the show like this? It would be the end of his career.

Suddenly something white caught Max's attention. It made him smile. He reached into the box and pulled out . . . Maxine Baby!

The audience jumped to its feet and applauded wildly. There were cheers and whistles. And this time Max took a long, low bow.

Everyone crowded around him.

"Max, you were magnificent," said Mr. Healy. He handed Max a five-dollar bill.

"I'm sure you'll be getting lots of calls after today,"

said Mrs. Healy. "You really know how to entertain children."

What Mrs. Healy had just said reminded Max of what Walter had told him: "Your goal as a magician is to entertain your audience." And that's what Max had done. He needed to practice more, he knew. Much more. So that nothing—not even Rosalie—could mix him up.

"You were great," said Austin. "You were the funniest."

"You really pulled it off," said Gordy.

Max looked at Gordy and Austin. He gave Maxine Baby a hug. "With a little help from my friends," he said. "I guess if I don't make it as a magician, I can always become a comedian."

More adventures of
Max Malone and his friends

Max Malone
and the Great Cereal Rip-off

Max Malone Makes a Million

Max Malone, Superstar